STRONGER TOGETHER

A COVID Super Hero Adventure

WRITTEN BY
CATHY BAINE

ILLUSTRATED BY
AMANDA COULSON

For Mom and Dad, you really are 'Super Hero' parents.

For William and Alice, you make our hearts sing.
—Grandma and Nanny

To JD & BF for the hours of editing, advice and tech support.

ISBN: 978-1-09836-625-4

Text copyright © 2020 by Cathy Baine
Illustrations copyright © 2020 by Amanda Coulson
All rights reserved.

No part of this publication may be reproduced in whole or in part, or stored in a retrieval system, or transmitted in any form, or by any means, electronic, mechanical, graphic or photocopying, recording or otherwise, without written permission of the author, Cathy Baine. The author, Cathy Baine, may be reached via email at clbaine57@gmail.com.

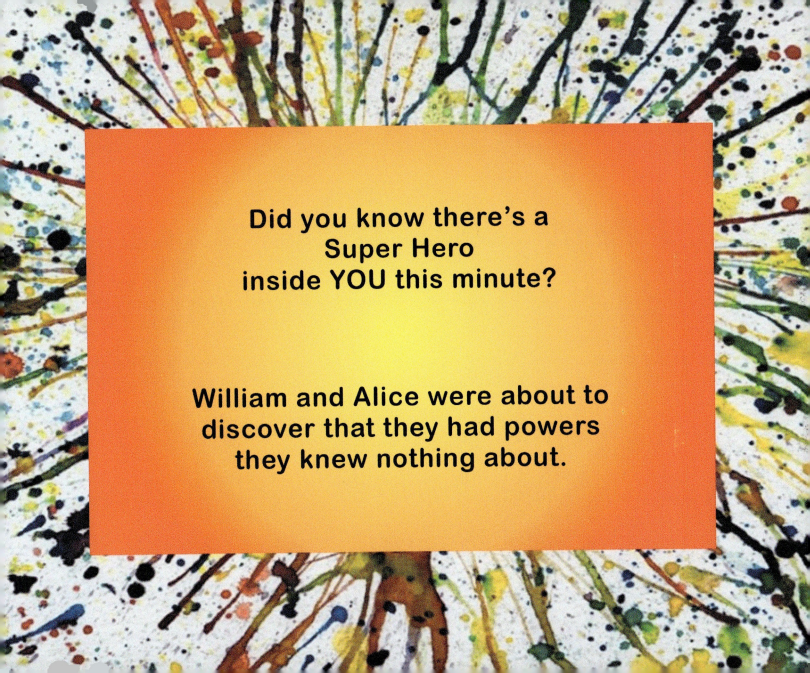

Did you know there's a
Super Hero
inside YOU this minute?

William and Alice were about to discover that they had powers they knew nothing about.

William was not afraid of anything.

Spooky things fascinated him. He spent hours drawing and colouring ghosts and zombies.

William would dream up scary plays, dress in costumes, and read books about Halloween all year long.

William was 5.

Alice was William's sister.

She enjoyed making people laugh. Her favourite game was Copy Me.

Alice loved the Imagination Box. She dressed up as a princess, a doctor, and even a strawberry. She could pretend to be anything she wanted.

Alice was excited to sing, have dance parties and play the drums. Music made her happy.

Alice was 2.

Both William and Alice looked forward to sleepovers at Grandma and Grandpa's house.

They would colour, have dance parties, and eat their favourite snacks. Some days they even had screen time. Grandma always read extra books at bedtime.

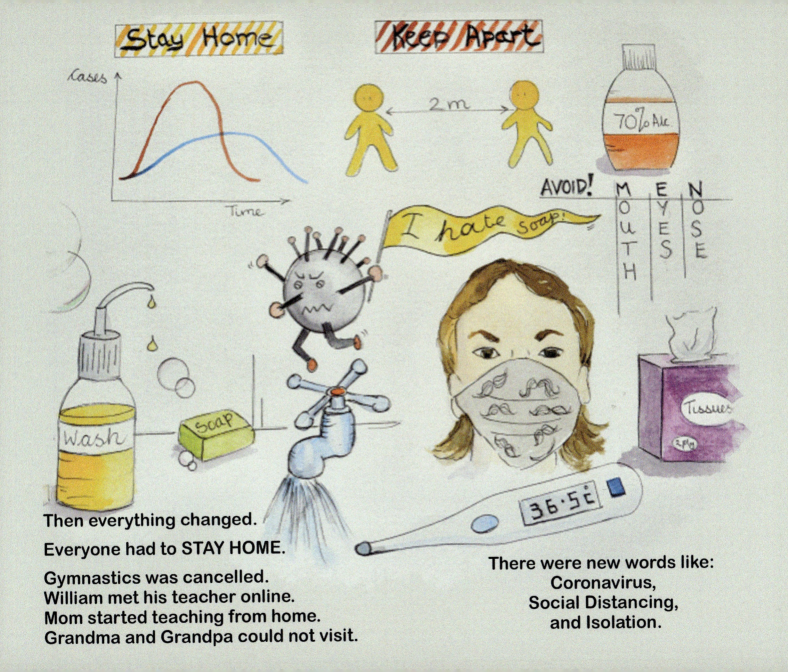

At first, it was fun to stay home. Every day a new craft project or LEGO challenge was completed.

They spent countless hours in Dad's music studio entertaining themselves with guitars and drums. Composing songs was their speciality.

Hand washing with scrubbing and sudsing was part of everything they did. Their hands felt like crocodile skin.

BE CREATIVE

Lots of spare time? Needing some Hope? Imagination will help you cope.

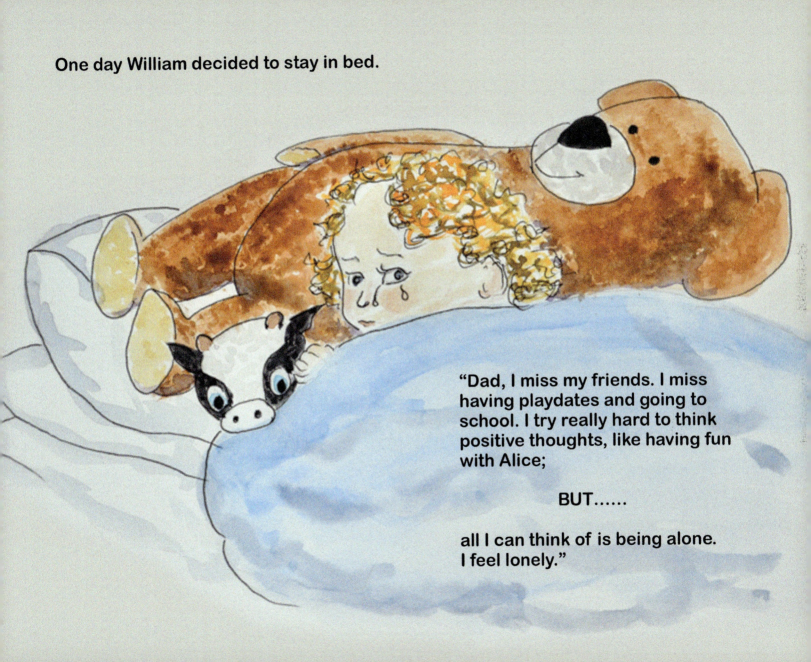

Dad said, "Have I told you about the COVID Super Heroes? It's all about a time when a dangerous villain caused destruction all over the world."

He called for Mom and Alice to come close.

"This is a story about four super heroes who used their super powers to help people who were feeling sad, lonely and worried…"

Dad showed them what to do. He stomped his feet two times, twirled in a circle and put both hands on his hips:

"Super Heroes Stand Strong! I am

With my shield of protection, I keep everyone healthy."

William and Alice could hardly believe their eyes.

Mom stomped her feet two times, twirled in a circle and reached her fist in the air:

"Super Heroes Stand Strong! I am

I use my lightning speed to avoid danger before it happens."

Would you like to be Super Heroes too?" she asked William and Alice.

"All you have to do is stomp your feet two times, twirl in a circle and strike a SuperHero pose. Then say the power words

'Super Heroes Stand Strong!'"

William's eyes sparkled with excitement as he went first.

He stomped his feet two times, twirled in a circle and posed.

"Super Heroes Stand Strong!"

Mom said, "You are the

On super hero quests, you have the ability to be invisible."

It was Alice's turn.
She stomped her feet two times,
twirled in a circle and posed.

"Super Heroes Stand Strong!"

Dad said, "You are the

Essential Warrior

You have incredible strength.
You can climb over any
obstacles in your way."

"We are the COVID Super Heroes."

"What do we do?" asked William.

"We fight the devious CoronaVirus using our super powers. We bring joy and keep everyone SAFE because

WE ARE ALL IN THIS TOGETHER".

"Now we must all practise the top-secret, confidential action (that only we know)."

Then the Fearless Phantom surprised everyone by delivering the special drawings and notes using his powers of invisibility.

It felt good to be kind to other people.

WE ARE ALL IN THIS TOGETHER.

SHOW EMPATHY

We'll send you pictures and make you smile.
Please stay home and don't stockpile.

The days slipped by and the sun shone brighter. The weather became warmer.

William and Alice played dress-up and had tea parties. They played hide-and-seek in the yard and attempted daredevil stunts on their bikes.

Things felt almost NORMAL.

Everyone worked together. The smell of freshly baked sourdough bread filled the house. They made chocolate cake and fruit popsicles.

Rainbow coloured balloons and streamers decorated the room. Party invitations were sent to friends, aunts, uncles, cousins, Grandmas, Grandpas, and Nanny and Grandad.

The days went on. Supreme Isolator took his shield of protection and bravely went out to buy groceries and toilet paper.

Agent Quarantine worked from home and used her lightning speed to be in many places at once.

Essential Warrior climbed as high as she could on every treacherous obstacle.

Fearless Phantom practiced his invisible, stealthy sneaking skills.

Things felt ALMOST NORMAL.

Visiting with Grandma
and Grandpa on the
computer was not the
same as seeing them
in person.

William said to Alice,
"I know we have to keep
Grandma and Grandpa
safe;

BUT......

all I can think of is fun-filled
sleepovers and searching
for ladybugs."

"This is a job for
the COVID
Super Heroes!"

Mom, Dad, Alice, and William stomped their feet two
times, twirled in a circle and struck their super hero pose.
They said the power words:
"Super Heroes Stand Strong!"
and performed the top-secret, confidential action
(that only they knew).

Agent Quarantine used her supersonic speed to take everyone to Grandma and Grandpa's house.

They brought their fluorescent sidewalk chalk. Bright, inspiring pictures soon covered the driveway and sidewalks.

Essential Warrior climbed an enormous tree in the yard to hang a sign that said,

"WE MISS YOU."

ALWAYS BELIEVE

Gradually things began to improve. The Coronavirus was less of a threat.

Restaurants and schools reopened.
Everyone scheduled a haircut.
Mom travelled back to work.
Dad resumed teaching guitar.

When days seem dark and very long,
Know light will return and you'll be strong.

The Super Heroes needed a NEW NORMAL.

They decided to spend more time doing things that made them happy.

They had more family time and lots of Super Hero time.

They baked decadent treats and delivered them to fire halls and police stations. They entertained seniors with songs and long conversations.

They had friendly chats with the grocery clerks when shopping for food.

They shovelled sidewalks on freezing winter days; and volunteered at the local animal shelter.

Their positive attitudes brought other people joy.

We'll help you thrive in any weather
Because we are Stronger Together.